DO YOU ENJOY BEING FRIGHTENED?

**WOULD YOU RATHER HAVE
NIGHTMARES
INSTEAD OF SWEET DREAMS?**

**ARE YOU HAPPY ONLY WHEN
SHAKING WITH FEAR?**

CONGRATULATIONS ! ! ! !

YOU'VE MADE A WISE CHOICE.

**THIS BOOK IS THE DOORWAY
TO ALL THAT MAY FRIGHTEN YOU.**

GET READY FOR

**COLD, CLAMMY SHIVERS
RUNNING UP AND DOWN YOUR SPINE!**

**NOW, OPEN THE DOOR–
IF YOU DARE !!!!**

Shivers™

MADNESS AT THE MALL

M. D. Spenser

Paradise Press, Inc.

Plantation, Florida

For Lindsay and Frank

Published by Paradise Press, Inc. by arrangement with River Publishing, Inc. All
right, title and interest to the "SHIVERS" logo and design are owned by River
Publishing, Inc. No portion of the "SHIVERS" logo and design may be reproduced
in part or whole without prior written permission from River Publishing, Inc. An
application for a registered trademark of the "SHIVERS" logo and design is pend-
ing with the Federal Patent and Trademark office.

ISBN 1-57657-153-X

EXCLUSIVE DISTRIBUTION BY PARADISE PRESS, INC.
30780

Cover Illustration by Eddie Roseboom

Printed in the U.S.A.

Chapter One

Frank was psyched.

He had lived in San Mateo, California, for only two weeks and already he had a date. Well, maybe not a real date, but she had agreed to meet him at the mall to see a horror movie.

She was Deanna Fields. And man was she cool.

Deanna was in Frank's sixth grade class. She sat two rows in front of him. From the first day he started at San Mateo Middle School, Frank had been watching her.

Deanna had beautiful black hair, big brown eyes, and a pretty smile. It didn't hurt that she was one of the smartest kids in the class, too. Frank had always liked smart girls.

Back home in Massachusetts, he had his first crush on a girl named Debbie Fox. She was really smart and pretty too. He figured he had pretty good taste in women.

When Frank's dad told him that they were moving

to California, Debbie Fox was one of the main reasons he didn't want to go. He had daydreams of going out with her when they got older.

Now that would never happen.

He hadn't wanted to leave his friends or his school, either. He had lived his whole life in Massachusetts and it had seemed strange to think about living so far away.

But now that his family was settling in, California seemed pretty cool.

And Deanna Fields lived here. Life goes on!

Frank had thought about asking Deanna to meet him at the movies all week long but he had been too nervous.

Finally, at lunch on Friday, he got up the nerve.

She was sitting at a large picnic table with a bunch of other girls. Frank took a deep breath and walked over to the table.

"Hi, Deanna," he mumbled.

"Did you say something, Frank?" Deanna asked.

"Yeah, I, uh, was just, uh, wondering if you'd seen the new, uh, horror film that's, uh, playing at the uh, mall," Frank stuttered. He couldn't believe how nervous he felt.

Deanna's friends giggled, but she didn't seem to

hear them.

"No," she replied. "I really want to see it, though. I love scary movies."

She was so calm and cool. She sounded as if she was totally relaxed. Why, Frank wondered, couldn't he just chill out?

He took a deep breath.

"Well, would you like to see it tonight?" he asked. "I'm going to the eight o'clock show."

"Sounds great!" Deanna said. "I'll meet you out front fifteen minutes before show time."

"You're crazy, Deanna," said her friend Sharon, who was known around school as a real goody-goody. "I would never see a scary movie at that mall. I'd be too freaked."

Frank hardly even heard Sharon's remark. He was so happy that Deanna had said yes. She was actually going to meet him at the movies! Wow!

California was quite a place.

Chapter Two

The rest of the school day seemed to drag.

Frank kept watching the clock, and that sure didn't make time pass any more quickly. But he couldn't help himself. He could barely even hear what was going on in class. He just kept staring at the clock, hoping the hands would move.

Finally, after an eternity, three o'clock rolled around.

As he was getting his backpack together, Frank felt a hand grip his shoulder. He froze.

"Frank, can I see you before you leave today?" Mrs. Gallie asked.

Mrs. Gallie was Frank's teacher.

It is never a good sign when your teacher wants to talk to you at the end of the day. Frank had been doing pretty well in school so far. He wasn't sure what this could be about.

Slowly, he shuffled past the kids who were heading out and made his way to Mrs. Gallie's desk.

"Frank," she said. "I'm disappointed to see that you didn't complete your science project on time. Did you forget that it was due today?"

The science project! Frank couldn't believe he had forgotten about it. Completely! He had been so preoccupied with Deanna all week that it had totally slipped his mind.

"I'm really sorry Mrs. Gallie," he said. "I can't believe I forgot about it. I'm not usually like that."

"Well, Frank, according to the letter I got from your previous teacher, you generally do very well in school," Mrs. Gallie said. "I don't want to see you developing bad work habits here. It's important that you do your assignments and hand them in on time."

"Yes, Mrs. Gallie," Frank replied. "I have no idea why I forgot."

There was no way he was going to tell his teacher that a girl was distracting him from his school work!

"I'm going to send a note home to your parents about this," Mrs. Gallie continued. "The note says that I expect you to turn in the science project on Monday. Please show the note to your parents, have them sign it, and bring it back to me with the completed work on Monday."

"I will, Mrs. Gallie."

"And, Frank, I hope this is the last time we run into this problem," Mrs. Gallie said.

This was just great. Two weeks in a new school and he had already messed up.

Mom and Dad were not going to like this at all.

Chapter Three

From his new house, Frank could ride his bike to school. Back in Massachusetts he'd had to take the bus. He had hated that.

These past two weeks, he had loved the freedom of going to and from school on his bike.

But today, the ride wasn't quite the same. It felt as if it was all uphill.

As he rode home, Frank could feel Mrs. Gallie's note burning in his back pocket. How was he going to explain to his parents that he had been so concerned with asking Deanna to the movies that he had just plain forgotten his science project?

Frank's dad worked as an engineer designing buildings. He had done work on the new mall here. Science was his favorite subject.

This was not going to be easy.

Frank turned into his driveway and left his bike just inside the gate to his yard. He had to admit that their yard here was far more beautiful than their yard had been back home.

Things in California seemed to bloom and stay green for a really long time.

It was just past Thanksgiving. When they had left Massachusetts last month, the leaves had already turned and fallen from the trees. Here some things were just starting to fade; others were still blooming beautifully.

He went around to the back door. As he walked inside, he could hear his mother talking on the phone.

Tom, his little brother, was sitting at the kitchen table eating cookies. Tom was in third grade and he got home from school earlier than Frank.

"Hi, Frank!" Tom said. "Mom baked our favorite cookies today. They're still warm."

Oh, to be eight years old and have your happiness based on what kind of cookies Mom made.

"I'm not hungry, Squirt," Frank said.

"Don't call me squirt!"

"I'll call you anything I want."

"*Mom*!" Tom shouted. "Frank's calling me names."

Mrs. Chase walked into the kitchen looking angry.

"Is it too much to ask for you boys to keep it down while I'm on the phone?" she demanded. "You are old enough to know better."

"But Mom, Frank is calling me names," Tom whined.

"Frank, please leave your brother alone."

"Sorry, Mom," Frank said. He knew he would be in enough hot water about the science project. No sense making things worse.

"By the way guys, that was your dad on the phone," their mother said. "One of the department heads at his office is having a small dinner party tonight, and we're invited."

"Bor-ing!" Tom said.

"Don't worry, buddy," Mrs. Chase said. "You guys are not on the guest list. Dad and I will be leaving around seven-thirty. We probably won't be home too late. What do you say we run to the video store and rent a movie for you guys to watch tonight?"

Tonight?

Frank was devastated. If his parents went out and left him home with Tom, how could he meet Deanna at the movies?

This was not turning out to be a good day.

9

Chapter Four

"Do you *have* to go, Mom?" Frank asked.

"Well, yes," she said. "The party is kind of in our honor. You know, to help Daddy and me get to know some of the other company people. What's the matter? You're not worried about being alone, are you?"

Frank and Tom had been staying home alone at night for a whole year. Back in Massachusetts, Frank's fifth grade class had taken a CPR and baby-sitting workshop. Afterwards, his parents had stopped hiring baby-sitters and started leaving him in charge.

He liked being home alone with Tom. For some reason, they got along much better when their mom and dad weren't around.

"Of course I'm not scared to be alone," he said. "It's just that I had other plans for tonight."

"What kind of plans?" Mrs. Chase asked.

"I made plans to meet a friend from school at the mall and see a movie," Frank said. He tried to sound nonchalant but he knew his voice was betraying him.

"I'm sorry, honey," his mother said. "Why don't you call him and ask him to meet you tomorrow instead?"

"I can't," Frank said gloomily. "I don't have her phone number."

He realized too late that he had said the word "her."

"*Her*?" Tom asked gleefully. "Did you say *her* phone number? Frank's got a girlfriend! Frank's got a girlfriend!"

"That's enough, Tom," Mrs. Chase interrupted. "Why don't you go read a book for a while."

Whenever their mom or dad wanted to speak to one of the boys, they always sent the other one off to read a book. It was a sure sign that the conversation was about to get juicy.

Tom left the room a trifle unwillingly.

"So, Frank, you asked a girl to the movies?" Mrs. Chase asked.

"Please don't make a big deal out of it Mom," Frank said. "She's just someone in my class who seems nice. We both wanted to see the same movie so we agreed to meet at the mall tonight."

Now that Tom was out of the room, Frank thought this would be a good opportunity to tell his mom about the science project.

"By the way, Mom, I had a science project to do this week and I kind of like forgot about it," he blurted out as fast as he could. "Mrs. Gallie sent you this note. You have to sign it so I can bring it back to school on Monday. I'm really sorry."

He handed his mother the note and waited nervously while she read it.

"The note says that Mrs. Gallie is disappointed in you," his mother said. "I don't mind telling you that I am, too. You never had these problems back in Massachusetts. Does your interest in this girl have anything to do with this?"

Wasn't that just like a mother to jump to conclusions? She was right, of course, but how did *she* know that?

"No Mom, I just forgot about it," Frank said. "I'll get it done this weekend. I promise."

"I guess it's just as well that you'll be staying home with your little brother tonight," Mrs. Chase said. "Boys who don't do science projects don't get to go to the movies."

She turned and left the kitchen. As she walked out the kitchen door, she nearly tripped over Tom.

Of course, Frank thought. The little guy had

known that something juicy was going to be discussed, and he had waited right around the corner so he could listen in.

"Come on, Sherlock," he heard his mother joke. "Looks like it's your choice at the video store."

That's just great, Frank said to himself. I get stuck baby-sitting instead of going to the movies with Deanna. And to top it off, the twerp gets to choose the video.

Life stinks!

Chapter Five

Frank was up in his room sulking when Tom and his mother returned from the video store. He was trying to figure out what he would say to Deanna at school on Monday.

She would probably hate him. What if she never spoke to him again? If only he knew her phone number.

There was a knock on his bedroom door.

"Come in," Frank grunted.

"Hey, Frank, guess what movie I rented?" Tom said.

"I don't know and I don't care," Frank replied.

"Come on, Frank, guess!"

"Listen, Squirt," Frank said. "Whatever you rented, it couldn't possibly compare with the movie that's playing at the mall. Just leave me alone."

"I don't know why you'd even want to see a scary movie at that mall," Tom said.

It suddenly hit Frank that he had heard almost

those exact words earlier in the day.

"What do you mean?" he asked.

"Well, the other day at school, some kids were talking about the new mall," Tom said. "They said it's haunted."

"Don't be ridiculous," Frank said. "How could a *mall* be haunted?"

"These kids told me there used to be a pet cemetery right where they built the mall," Tom said. "They said bulldozers came in and dug up the graves without even moving the dead animals first. Then they just built the mall right on top of them!"

"That's gross," Frank said.

"Some of these kids think the ghosts of the dead animals haunt the mall," Tom said.

"Well, I don't believe it," Frank said. "Dad worked on building that mall. He would never agree to that kind of plan. Besides, there's no such thing as ghosts."

"Well maybe there is and maybe there isn't," Tom said. "But I'm not planning on going near that mall ever again. Especially not at night."

Chapter Six

As Frank's mother got dressed to go out, Frank got dinner for himself and Tom.

Frank was quite good at cooking but tonight he was less than enthusiastic. He popped two trays of frozen macaroni and cheese into the microwave.

While he waited for the food to cook, he took down the telephone book.

Back in Massachusetts practically every town had its own telephone book. But here, the phone book included the whole county.

Frank figured he had better at least *try* to find Deanna's phone number. If he called and canceled, he'd have a chance to talk to her. Maybe she'd understand and they could reschedule.

He didn't know her parents' names or their address, but at least he knew her last name. He thumbed through the Fs looking for "Fields." It was worth a try.

There were forty-four listings under the name

Fields. He could not possibly call forty-four numbers and ask for Deanna.

The bell rang on the microwave. Dinner was ready. Maybe food would help him think of a solution to his problem.

"Tom, come on in here," he called. "Dinner's ready."

Tom was caught up in a computer game in the next room. Frank had his own computer in his room. He had gotten it for his birthday last year. But Tom used the family computer, which was set up in a little alcove off the kitchen. He was playing Animal Pursuit — for a change.

"Just a minute!" he called. "I'm almost through the last level. . . . Aw, I got eaten by a bear."

He came into the kitchen and plopped onto a stool at the counter.

"The bears are the hardest predators to escape from," he said. "I'd hate to meet a bear in real life."

"I thought you loved animals," Frank said.

"I love cats and dogs and guinea pigs," Tom replied. "Not grizzly bears. After all what harm could a pet do you?"

Chapter Seven

When Frank finished eating, he still hadn't come up with a solution.

He wanted to see Deanna so badly that he couldn't think straight. He wanted to meet her at the mall.

"Hey, Tom," he said finally, "how would you like to go on a secret mission with me?"

"I'm listening," Tom said.

Frank and Tom had played together a lot when they were younger, mostly because there weren't a lot of other kids living near them. But in the last couple of years, Frank had outgrown the games Tom liked to play.

That had made Tom sad. So Frank knew Tom would jump at the chance to be included in one of his schemes.

"What do you say, we sneak out tonight and check out this haunted mall story?" Frank asked. "We'll be like real spies."

"Are you crazy?" Tom said. "Didn't I just tell you

I would never go near that place at night?"

"Come on, Sherlock," Frank said. "Aren't you just a little curious about this haunting stuff? Besides, I told you, there's no such thing as ghosts."

"Well if there's no such thing as ghosts, why check it out?" Tom asked.

Frank saw his plan crumbling. Maybe Tom was finally growing up. He wasn't so easy to manipulate anymore. Maybe Frank would have to tell him the truth.

He couldn't see any other way. He took a deep breath and plunged ahead.

"OK, listen Tom," he said. "I'm in a jam and I need your help. Tease me if you want, but I made plans to meet this girl at the mall and I have no way to reach her to cancel the plans. Just come with me to the mall, let me talk to her and then we'll come home. OK?"

"What's it worth to you?" Tom asked.

"I'll give you half of my allowance this week," Frank offered.

"I want it all," Tom said.

"Fine," Frank said. "I appreciate this. You're a pal."

But he was thinking that his nice little brother had turned into a cunning little twit.

Chapter Eight

As the boys were cleaning up their dinner plates, they heard the garage door open. Their dad was just getting home from work.

It was just past seven o'clock. He would barely have time to jump in the shower and change for the party. He rushed in through the kitchen door.

"Hey guys!" he boomed. "How was your day?"

Mr. Chase was a large, cheery, easy-going man. He rarely got angry.

"Hey, Dad," Tom said. "Some kids at school said the mall you helped build is right on top of a pet cemetery. Is that true?"

Frank shot Tom a nasty look. How could he bring up the mall now? What if his Dad figured out what they were planning to do?

Relax, he told himself. You're just being paranoid.

"Well, Tom, yes there was a pet cemetery there before," Mr. Chase replied. "But I was told that all the graves were moved before construction began."

"Where did they move them to?" Tom asked.

"I don't know," Mr. Chase said. "Some other pet cemetery, I suppose. That all happened before I became involved. Hey, I'd love to stay and chat with you guys about dead animals but your mom will kill me if we're late for this party."

Mr. Chase left the room. Frank shot Tom a knowing look.

"I *told* you Dad wouldn't have anything to do with building a mall on top of dead pets," he said.

Their parents, dressed in their good clothes, rushed out of the house at seven-thirty, tossing waves and instructions over their shoulders as they left.

They were notorious for forgetting something and running back into the house after they got halfway down the block. Frank waited a few minutes to be sure they were gone for good.

"Come on, Tom," he said. "Let's get our bikes and get this over with."

Frank was not particularly happy about making this trip. As much as he wanted to see Deanna, he did *not* want to tell her he couldn't stay at the movies, and that he was standing her up.

He was almost sorry he had ever worked up the courage to ask her out in the first place.

Chapter Nine

It felt weird riding their bikes in the dark.

The boys were never allowed to bicycle at night. They were also not allowed to leave the house when their parents left them home alone.

They were breaking so many rules that Frank couldn't even count them all.

As long as we don't get caught, he thought, we'll be fine.

They rode in silence, keeping to the side streets. Frank figured they'd be less likely to be seen that way. He hoped they would not meet anyone they knew at the mall.

Lucky for us, he thought, that we don't know too many people in California yet.

He rode ahead. Tom, who had only learned to ride a two-wheeler last year, followed. He couldn't ride as fast as Frank. His bike was a lot smaller too.

Frank raced ahead, his hair flying in the wind, and leaned his way around a corner.

Behind him, he heard Tom let out a yell, followed by the unmistakable sound of metal hitting the pavement.

Frank stopped. He felt the ground rumbling. He saw the traffic light swaying madly.

He turned to find Tom lying in the street, his legs tangled in his bike.

"Are you OK?" Frank called out.

He ran over to his brother. Tom was a little shaken, but he seemed OK.

"That was so weird Frank," Tom said, getting up and dusting himself off. "Did you feel it?"

"You mean the ground shaking?" Frank asked.

"It knocked me right off my bike," Tom said.

"Well, little brother," Frank said. "I think we just experienced our first California earthquake."

"That couldn't have been an earthquake," Tom said. "It was so quick. I thought earthquakes were longer, and buildings fell and stuff."

"Hey, they can't all be major. California would have fallen into the ocean years ago," Frank said.

"That's a pleasant thought."

"Come on Tom," Frank said. "If you're not hurt, let's keep going."

Chapter Ten

They got to the mall a few minutes before eight.

Frank scanned the crowd, and saw Deanna waiting for him by the ticket window. She looked annoyed.

Frank told Tom to wait for him by the bike rack. He walked over to Deanna.

"Hi," Frank said.

"I thought you weren't coming," Deanna said. "The movie starts in a couple of minutes. Come on."

"Wait," Frank began. "I can't go in."

"Why not?"

"My parents had to go out and I have to stay home to baby-sit my little brother," Frank said. "I wanted to call you but I didn't know your phone number. Did you know there are forty-four 'Fields' in the phone book?"

"Where's your brother now?" Deanna asked. "You didn't leave him home alone, did you?"

"He's over there by the bikes," Frank said.

"Well," said Deanna, "why don't you just bring him in, too? Otherwise, I'll have to go in alone. And I really don't want to see this movie alone. In fact, I've never gone to the movies alone before. Ever."

"I really don't think I should," Frank said. "Tom's too young to see this movie. And we could get in a lot of trouble, too. Can't you just call your parents and ask them to come get you? I'll wait until they get here."

"They're not home," Deanna said. "They dropped me off and went downtown for dinner. They're picking me up after the movie is over." Deanna said.

Deanna sounded kind of upset. She looked it, too. And the last thing Frank wanted to do was upset her.

What a mess.

"I guess we can see it," Frank said reluctantly. "If we ride home right after it ends, I'm sure we'll beat my parents home."

"Thanks Frank," Deanna said. "I'd really be too scared to go to the movies by myself."

Frank waved Tom to come over and told him what was happening.

"But I don't want to go to a scary movie with you and some dumb girl," Tom said. "I'm telling Mom and Dad."

"If you tell, you can forget about getting my allowance," Frank said. "In fact, you can forget about getting *your* allowance, too, because I know where you stash it and I'll take it all."

"Fine," Tom said. "But I hope you get in so much trouble."

The three of them bought tickets and went inside to find seats.

Chapter Eleven

The theater was dark. It took their eyes some time to adjust, and they started to grope their way forward hoping they wouldn't step on somebody.

Finally, they found three good seats together, pretty near the front and right in the center.

Frank gave Tom money for popcorn and soda. This night was costing him a fortune.

Tom left, making his way slowly along the row of seats, toward the aisle. Frank was finally alone with Deanna.

He couldn't think of a single thing to say.

He thought about mentioning the weather, but that seemed dumb. He wondered whether he should compliment her clothes, but that seemed too forward. He considered asking how school had gone that day, but that seemed silly.

"I heard some kids think this mall is haunted," he blurted out finally. Immediately, he felt stupid for saying it.

"My friend Sharon thinks so," Deanna said. "Didn't you hear her when she said she wouldn't see a scary movie at this mall? Lots of the kids are *sure* the mall is haunted."

"But there's no such thing as ghosts," Frank said. "At least I don't think there is."

"Well, I've heard stories that strange things have happened here at night," Deanna said. "You know, after the mall closes. People say the spirits of the animals vandalize the place. The night cleaning crew got so spooked they walked off the job a couple of weeks ago. There was a story about it in the newspaper. In fact, they still haven't gone back to work."

"Seems unbelievable to me," said Frank.

Tom found his way back and plopped into his seat just as the movie began. It was called *Revenge of the Savages*.

It was a really gross movie, very gory. Body parts got ripped off and flung around. Blood spurted from the wounds. Tom spent a lot of time with his hands over his face.

Frank thought it was kind of funny. It was too bizarre to be believable.

He did like one thing about the movie, though.

Deanna kept burying her face in his shoulder. She couldn't watch the gross parts — and, fortunately for Frank, there were plenty of them.

By the time the movie ended, Frank had his arm around Deanna's shoulder. She seemed to like it. He felt so happy he had come to the mall tonight that he didn't even care if he got caught.

The credits rolled on the screen. Deanna stood up to leave.

Just then, the floor started to move and the seats began to shake. Deanna lost her balance and let out a scream.

Chapter Twelve

With a thump, Deanna landed right in Frank's lap.

Tom screamed. All over the theater, people yelled and ran for the doors. It was total mayhem.

"Don't panic," Frank said, shouting to be heard over the noise, confusion and screaming. "It's just another small earthquake. Just like the one we felt on our way over here. It's already over."

Deanna slid off of Frank's lap and stood up. The floor had stopped moving. It seemed to be over — for now. But she was still trembling all over.

Deanna had lived in California her whole life. She had been through many earthquakes and she knew a few things about them that Frank didn't.

For one thing, she knew that they were totally unpredictable.

At the back of the theater, people were pushing past each other to squeeze out the narrow doors. It was bedlam.

"Let's just stay here until the crowd thins out," Frank said. "No sense getting caught in the crush of bodies back there."

"I'm not staying here one more second," Deanna shrieked. "It's not safe in here."

Before Frank could stop her, she ran down the aisle and disappeared into the crowd.

"It's creepy in here Frank," Tom said, his voice quavering. "I want to leave too." He sounded really frightened.

Just then they felt another rumble.

Frank looked back at the massive crowd. People were falling all over each other trying to get out the door.

He didn't want to take his little brother out through that mob scene. It looked far less safe than staying put.

He looked around the theater for another way out.

Then he saw it, the orange lights glowing in the darkness. An emergency exit was right down front, under the movie screen.

"Come on Tom," he shouted, grabbing his brother's hand. "We're going out this way. If *this* isn't an emergency, I don't know what is!"

They ran to the front of the theater. A red sign said an alarm would sound if the door was opened. Tom covered his ears. Frank pushed hard on the handle.

The door flew open. No alarm sounded. Frank and Tom hurried through the door and found themselves in a dark hallway.

The door clicked shut behind them.

Small red lights high on the wall glowed every twenty or thirty feet, but they didn't throw much light. Frank had trouble finding his way through the darkness.

"I wonder why the alarm didn't go off when we opened the door," Tom said.

"I don't know," Frank said. "Maybe the earthquake screwed up the mall's electrical system. Let's just get out of here."

He looked up and down the hallway.

He figured the main shopping part of the mall was to the right and the outside was to the left.

He checked his watch. It was nine thirty-five.

The shopping part of the mall would be closed by now. He decided to head left towards what he hoped would be the outside.

The two of them walked quickly down the hall. The light was so dim that they could only see a few feet in front of themselves as they went.

As he picked his way through the dim light, Frank wondered how Deanna had made out in the crush of the crowd. He hoped she was OK.

Tom reached up and took hold of Frank's hand. It had been a couple of years since he had done anything like that.

He must really be scared, Frank thought.

He had no time to worry about Deanna now. He had gotten himself and his little brother into quite a mess.

If they could just get outside to their bikes, though, they might still make it home before their parents arrived.

Chapter Thirteen

After what seemed an eternity, Frank and Tom reached the end of the hallway.

There they saw another heavy emergency door with a red handle and a warning about an alarm sounding if it was opened.

Frank pushed on the handle. Nothing happened. The door didn't move.

He had expected it to open easily, like the first one.

He leaned into it with all his weight. Still nothing.

"Give me a hand with this door, Tom," he said, "I can't get it open."

Frank pushed in the handle while he and his brother pressed their bodies against the door and pushed with their legs.

It wouldn't budge.

"*Now* what are we going to do?" Tom said. His voice had that whiny sound that drove their mom crazy.

"Listen, Tom," Frank said. "We'll get out of here OK, but you have to stop whining. Can you do that?"

"I'll try."

After giving the door one last shove — and finding that it still would not open — Frank took Tom's hand and led him back down the long, dark corridor.

"Maybe the electrical system messed up the lock on the door the way it messed up the alarm," Frank said.

It didn't really matter *why* the door wouldn't open. Frank was just talking to fill the silence. He was beginning to get worried and he didn't want to upset Tom.

When they got back to the door to the theater, Frank figured they'd better just go back into the theater and leave the way they had come in. Surely the crowed had thinned out by now.

He reached to press in the red handle to open the door — and let out a gasp.

There was no handle!

The door was completely flat on this side. A sign read "No Access." This door could only be opened from the inside.

"Well this is just great," Frank said.

He looked at Tom and saw tears welling up in his eyes.

"Please don't cry, Tom," he said. "It's no big deal. We'll just go down the other way and find another door. Come on."

He held out his hand, but Tom wouldn't take it.

Instead Tom began pounding on the door with both fists and screaming at the top of his lungs.

"Help us!" he yelled. "Let us in! Is anybody in there? Can you hear me? *He-e-e-l-p*!"

Frank grabbed Tom around the waist and pulled him away from the door. Tom fell silent. The two of them put their ears to the door and listened intently.

They heard nothing. Not a sound.

Again Tom pounded and shouted. This time, Frank joined him, banging and shouting at the top of his lungs. Together they kicked and slammed and hammered and screamed.

Then they stopped and listened. Still nothing.

This time when Frank held out his hand, Tom took it.

Without a word, they turned and began walking in the other direction down the dark hallway.

<u>Chapter Fourteen</u>

Unlike the first hallway, this one was not straight.
It turned left, then right, then right again, and left.

They had turned so many times that Frank could
no longer figure out what direction they were heading in.

Along the way they passed more doors. But, like
the other one, these had no handles on their side.

Each had a sign saying the same thing — "No Access." Each time they read it, it felt like a slap in the face.

What have I gotten us into, Frank wondered. If
only I hadn't dragged Tom out here tonight!

All this over a girl. I just may be done with girls
for a while.

Then Frank remembered how nice it had felt when
Deanna had buried her face in his shoulder.

Nice, sure — but had it been worth all this trouble? He'd have to give that some serious thought.

But not now. Now he could think about only one
thing. How was he going to get his little brother out of

here, and back home before his parents returned?

He checked his watch. Nine-fifty. He had never fully appreciated the light on his watch before. It sure came in handy now.

His parents had given him the watch last year for his birthday. It lit up, and told the date, the altitude — and it had a compass, too.

Why hadn't he thought about that sooner?

Maybe the compass would help him navigate these hallways!

He knew they had parked their bikes in the parking area on the north side of the mall. According to the compass, they were now heading south.

The main mall area, Frank figured, would be to the west, or to their right. The boys took the next right turn they found.

Soon they came to another door. Frank was about to walk right by, but Tom called out, "Look, Frank! This one has a handle!"

Frank couldn't believe his eyes. Not only did this door have a handle, but it was a regular kind of handle, not some emergency handle with a warning about an alarm.

This wasn't an emergency exit. It was an ordinary door.

Frank pushed down on the handle. The door opened easily. Frank breathed a sigh of relief.

Then he looked at what lay ahead, and his relief gave way to panic.

Chapter Fifteen

Frank and Tom stepped through the door and found themselves in the mall.

But it didn't look anything like the way they'd ever seen it before.

It was quite dark, eerie, and deserted.

Frank looked around.

All the shops had metal gates drawn across their entrances. The escalators stood still. The fountains had been turned off.

Everything lay still and gloomy and quiet. Frank felt the hair on the back of his neck stand up. The whole place looked incredibly creepy.

Frank had only been in the mall a few times. He wasn't sure of the whole layout, but he had a general idea about where things were.

He checked his compass. North was to their right.

Holding Tom's hand, he began walking that way. That had to be where the movie theater was. That was where he thought they would have the best chance of getting out.

Even though it felt creepy, it also seemed kind of cool to walk through the mall alone at night. If his mother could do her shopping like this, she'd be psyched. No crowds, no lines, no delays.

And no cashiers. Just help yourself to what you need.

OK, Frank, he told himself. Enough fantasizing. You've got to keep a clear head and get yourself and your little brother home. Soon.

It was ten p.m. He hoped his parents were having a good time at the dinner party. The more fun they had, the later they would stay.

Anyway, as the guests of honor, he knew they wouldn't be the first ones to leave.

He hoped they hadn't called home to check on him. But there was no sense in worrying about that now. There would be plenty of time to make up excuses later.

He quickened his pace.

"Slow down, Frank," Tom whined. "You're going too fast, I'm getting a cramp."

"Sorry, Tom. I just want to get out of here as quickly as we can."

"Mom and Dad are really going to let you have it

this time," Tom said.

"Shut up, twerp."

How was it, Frank wondered, that with one small remark his little brother could make all his protective, big-brother feelings evaporate?

One minute he was looking out for Tom, worried about him, concerned that he not get scared. Then the next minute he wanted to knock him to the ground.

That's just brotherly love, I guess, he told himself.

They passed the video arcade. It felt weird to see it so dark and quiet. No flashing lights. No electronic sounds. No clamor of kids or clanking of coins.

The brothers paused at the gate covering the entrance and peered into the dark arcade.

Suddenly, they felt it again.

The ground shook. Harder than before. The metal gate shuddered and rattled in their hands.

Inside the arcade, the games sprang to life. Lights flashed, bells rang, engines roared. Every one of those video games seemed suddenly to have been turned on.

But the games weren't just on. It looked as if they were being *played*.

Then Frank heard a scream.

He turned to look down at Tom — and realized Tom's face was at eye-level with his own!

The gate to the video arcade was rising, and Tom was still holding on.

"Let go of the gate Tom," Frank shouted. "Let go!"

Frank grabbed the back of Tom's jeans. Tom let go and fell on top of Frank. The two of them crumbled to the floor in a heap.

It took Frank only a second to realize what had happened, and what it could mean to them.

"The earthquake must have set off the electrical system again," he shouted. "Maybe all of the gates have been released. Let's go!"

He jumped up, dragged Tom to his feet, and the two of them raced towards the north entrance of the mall.

Chapter Sixteen

The floor shifted under them as they ran, and they had trouble keeping their balance.

But soon the rumbling stopped. With their hearts thumping in their throats, they sprinted through the gloom toward the north side entrance.

They heard gates opening and closing all around them. Frank hoped the gate to the main entrance was opening, too.

"What if the gate isn't open?" Tom cried.

"Just keep running, Tom!" said Frank. " We'll see when we get there!"

Frank recognized the stores. They had almost reached the entrance. He urged Tom on. Running as fast as they could, with their hair flying, they rounded the last corner.

The gate was just coming down.

As if they were sliding into home plate with the winning run, both of them hit the ground and tried to slide under the gate.

But they were too late!

Frank got one leg under before the bars of the gate clanked shut. Tom's body rammed against the bars.

For a moment, the boys lay there, stunned. Neither one moved.

Slowly, Tom got to his feet.

"Now what Frank?" he asked.

Frank didn't answer. He tried to stand up, but he couldn't.

"My leg is stuck under the gate," he said. "I can't move!"

Just then, dim lights came on all over the corridor.

"Must be emergency lights or something," Tom said.

"My pants are caught on the gate," Frank said. "I'll have to tear them to get my leg out!"

His leg was stuck between the bars of the gate. The bars had pierced his jeans, nailing them to the floor.

"Oh, man, is Mom ever going to kill you!" Tom said.

"I could hardly get into any more trouble than I'm in already," Frank said. "A torn pair of jeans isn't going to make much difference now."

He grabbed his jeans where they were caught on

the gate, and yanked as hard as he could. Finally, the denim gave way and his jeans ripped free of the gate.

But Frank still couldn't get his leg back through the gate. His foot wouldn't fit between the bars.

"What am I going to do?" he wailed.

"Try taking off your shoe," Tom suggested.

Frank reached his arm through the bars and wriggled his sneaker off. Gingerly, he managed to ease his foot back through the gate.

As Frank sat there putting his shoe back on, it hit him that he had just escaped a really close call. The gate could have pierced his leg instead of just tearing his pants.

He felt pretty lucky.

Then he remembered that they were still trapped inside the mall.

I guess, he said to himself grimly, lucky isn't exactly the right word.

Chapter Seventeen

"Now what are we going to do?" Tom asked.

"I'm not sure," Frank replied. "Give me a minute to think this through."

What would Dad do in a situation like this, Frank wondered. He's very scientific. He would think logically and calmly. He would assess the situation and come up with a plan.

Frank made a mental list of things he knew about their situation. First of all, they appeared to be the only ones in the mall.

Not good.

He also knew that they had experienced at least four small earthquakes since leaving home. Would there be more? Was this normal for earthquakes? What did a boy from Massachusetts know about earthquakes anyway?

Not much.

He also figured the earthquakes were responsible

for the gates opening and closing, the alarms not working right, and for the dim lights that just came on.

The last thing he knew was that if he didn't get them out of here soon, he would probably be grounded for the rest of his life!

He glanced around, trying to come up with some ideas.

The dim red emergency lights made it possible to see fairly well. There weren't many stores in this corridor by the movies — just a florist, a beauty salon and a candy store.

Suddenly, it struck him. The gate was open on the candy store! What a stroke of luck!

He knew he'd be breaking the law, but he figured these were special circumstances. Anyway, it would cheer up his little brother.

"Hey Tom," he said. "While I'm thinking of a plan, why don't you help yourself to some candy?"

He didn't have to suggest it twice. Tom saw the open gate, ran right in, grabbed a plastic bag and started stuffing it with his favorite candies.

Meanwhile, Frank did some serious thinking.

Maybe, he thought, their best plan would be to sit tight and wait for another quake. Then, if the gates opened, they'd be ready to scoot under and run right out the front doors.

He knew the front doors would be locked from the outside, but he figured he might be able to open them from the inside. It was worth a try.

He glanced at Tom, who was still grabbing fistfuls of goodies. What a pig, Frank thought. Tom had stuffed two sacks full of candy.

"Don't you think that's enough?" Frank called.

"What do you care?" Tom asked. "You're not paying for it are you?"

"No, but you couldn't possibly eat all of that," said Frank.

"Well, you never know how long we'll be stuck in here," Tom said. "And I don't want to starve to death."

"You're more likely to die of a sugar overdose," said Frank.

Tom was about to respond when suddenly he froze.

"Did you hear that?" he asked.

"Shhh. Let me listen," Frank said.

He couldn't quite make out the sound. It sounded like water running. He also thought he heard footsteps.

Maybe they weren't alone after all. Maybe someone else had been trapped inside with them.

Maybe they could get help!

Frank grabbed Tom's hand and took off down the corridor.

As they rounded the corner, they suddenly stopped dead in their tracks.

Chapter Eighteen

The boys stood staring at what they saw before them.

The enormous fountain, the focal point of this section of the mall, had been dark and still when they had passed it moments earlier.

Now it was lit up like the Fourth of July.

Lights blazed red and blue and white under the water. A shaft of light shot through the spray as the water burst towards the ceiling and curved back down to the base of the fountain. It was really beautiful.

It was also really strange.

Frank had never noticed the colored lights before. The fountain was always going and it was always lit up. But he could never remember seeing anything other than white lights.

"It looks so cool," said Tom. "I'd love to jump right in and swim."

"Don't you dare," Frank said. "You know you're

not supposed to swim in fountains."

"Yeah, well, I also know I'm not supposed to steal candy, but you told me to do *that*," answered Tom.

"Well, now I'm telling you *not* to," Frank said. "So *don't*."

But Tom seemed drawn to the fountain's beauty. He walked up to the edge of the fountain and leaned over. His face was inches from the sparkling water.

"Hey, Frank, have you got a penny?" he asked. "I bet it's extra special lucky to make a wish in a colorful fountain like this."

Frank couldn't believe his little brother wanted to wish on a coin at a time like this. But Frank figured it couldn't hurt, so he dug in his pocket for a penny.

"Here you go kid," he said. "I guess I don't have to tell you what to wish for."

"Of course not," Tom said. "I'm wishing for in-line skates for my birthday."

"You lame-brain," said Frank. "I figured you'd wish for us to get out of here."

"Make your own wish, then," said Tom. "I want new skates."

At the same time, each of them tossed a penny into the fountain. Tom leaned over the edge to see where his landed.

Frank stood beside him and watched with amazement.

As the pennies hit the water, they began to fizz. Within seconds, both of them had disappeared.

Frank grabbed Tom's shirt and yanked him away from the edge of the fountain.

"I don't think that's water at all," Frank said. "To eat through two copper pennies, that must be some kind of acid. And to think that you wanted to *swim* in there! That stuff would eat the skin right off of your bones!"

"Get me outta here," Tom whimpered.

"I'm trying," said Frank. "I'm trying."

Chapter Nineteen

Frank and Tom backed away from the fountain, staring at it as if it were possessed.

Then they turned and began walking further into the mall.

Suddenly Frank remembered that, when they had first heard the water, they had also heard the sound of footsteps.

"Hello!" he called. "Is anybody else in here?"

His voice echoed through the mall. Tom munched on candy.

"Hel-lo!" Frank called again. No one answered.

Frank looked at Tom and shrugged. Tom shrugged back. They started walking.

Then, suddenly, they heard it again.

They stopped and strained to hear, not moving a muscle, not daring to breathe.

There it was again. It did sound like footsteps, only muffled somehow, not sharp and clacky, like a man in business shoes or a woman wearing heels. It sounded more like the soft tread of someone wearing slippers.

And it sounded like it was coming from above.

In an instant, Frank rejected the idea of waiting by the front gates in case they opened again. If someone was in here with them, he wanted to know who or what they were dealing with.

He grabbed Tom and headed towards the escalators. They were turned off, as he had expected, but that didn't matter. He held Tom's hand and began bounding up the still metal steps.

Suddenly, they felt a jolt. The escalator began moving.

Tom turned and started down the escalator, even though the steps were moving upwards. Frank couldn't tell if his brother was playing or panicked.

"Tom, what are you doing?" Frank called.

The escalator began to speed up. Tom teetered, tried to catch himself, and fell.

The escalator picked up more speed.

Frank reached the top and stepped off. Then he heard his brother shout.

"Frank, help me!" Tom called, with panic in his voice. "This thing is going crazy. It's going too fast!"

"Get up on your feet, Tom," Frank shouted. "You

have to stand up!"

"I can't! My shoelace is stuck in the escalator!"

Frank jumped onto the escalator and, taking the steps two at a time, ran down to Tom.

He didn't have much time. The escalator was moving so fast that they would hit the top again in seconds.

Quickly, he reached down and started to untie Tom's sneaker.

Frantically, he picked at the laces with his fingernails, but they were knotted. He couldn't get them undone.

He looked up. They were only ten feet from the top, and moving fast.

He grabbed the sneaker and yanked.

"Pull, Tom, pull!" he shouted. "We've got to get your foot out of this thing."

Tom yanked as Frank held the sneaker with both hands.

Just as they hit the top, Tom's foot popped free and they scrambled off the escalator in the nick of time.

As they watched in horror, the escalator sucked the sneaker into the mechanism. The sneaker disappeared with a horrid, crunching sound.

Tom let out a gasp that almost sounded like a sob.

"That could have been my foot," he said. He gasped for breath and shivered.

Frank wiped his forehead and tried to collect himself. That had been a close call.

"Well, you're OK now," he said.

"It never would have happened if the darn thing hadn't sped up like that," said Tom. "This place is getting weirder by the minute. It's almost like the mall is . . . "

"Don't even say it," Frank interrupted. "I'm sure there are logical explanations for everything. The electrical system is whacked out from the earthquakes."

"Maybe, but look at the down escalator," said Tom.

Frank looked. It wasn't moving at all. But the up escalator was still going at double speed.

"How can that be?" asked Tom. "It's almost like something is trying to stop us from coming up here. Like it deliberately turned the escalator on to knock me over so I wouldn't make it."

"Maybe the escalators are just running on different electrical circuits," Frank said.

"But that doesn't explain the penny-eating fountain," replied Tom.

"Well, I can't explain that one," Frank said. "Unless the water served as an electrical conductor and somehow reacted with the copper in the pennies to make them dissolve. Dad's the science guy. We'll ask him about it."

"If we ever see him again," said Tom.

"Don't be so melodramatic," said Frank. "Since we're up here, we might as well take a look around."

"OK, but when we go back down, I'm taking the stairs."

Chapter Twenty

The second level of the mall was set up just like the first, except that there was no corridor over in the area of the movie theater, as there had been down below.

Frank figured this must be because the movie theater was two stories tall.

He and Tom walked in the opposite direction, heading away from the north side. The staircases were all on the south side of the mall, and Frank wanted to be sure they could get down fast if they needed to.

They stayed close together. Tom was holding Frank's hand again.

Frank felt nervous. He could tell Tom felt nervous, too. And wearing only one shoe probably added to Tom's apprehension. After all, he wouldn't be able to run very well, if they needed to.

Just then, Frank noticed that they were approaching an athletic shoe store. The store must have had a sale that day. Right on the other side of the gate stood a folding table piled high with all kinds of sneakers.

They had running shoes, basketball shoes, cross trainers, cleats and more. Some of the shoes had spilled onto the floor. It was a total mess. Frank guessed the earthquake must have had something to do with it.

"Hey, Tom," Frank said, "would you feel better if you had two shoes again?"

"Yeah, sure I would," Tom said. "Mom's going to kill me when she finds out I need new sneakers. These were practically brand new."

"Well, the way I see it, this mall owes you a pair of new sneakers," Frank said. "After all, it was their escalator that destroyed your other one. Right?"

Tom thought about this for perhaps half a second.

"What are you plotting?" he asked.

"See those shoes next to the table in there?" Frank asked. "See the black and white ones on the floor? They look about your size. If I reach through the gate with my leg, I'll bet I can get them for you."

"Isn't that like stealing?" Tom asked.

"Normally, it would be," Frank said. "But I think these are special circumstances."

Frank got down onto his stomach and tried to stick his right leg through the bars. They were close together. Just as he had before, Frank found that he needed to remove his shoe first.

With his shoe off, Frank was able to slip his leg through. He could easily reach the pair of shoes he was after!

The pair was tied together by the laces. This was going to be easier than he thought.

Frank twisted his foot and wrapped the laces over the top of his foot. Slowly he dragged his leg, with the shoes trailing, back towards the gate.

Suddenly, he felt the rumbling, the unmistakable shaking, and his heart leapt to his throat.

Another earthquake!

Tom screamed and dropped to the floor beside Frank. He grabbed at Frank's shirt and tried to pull him away from the gate. The shoelaces fell from Frank's foot as Tom pulled and the ground shook.

The gates began their familiar dance. They rose a few inches and fell back down. They rose a few more inches and fell back down.

Once again, Frank came close to getting his thigh pierced by the heavy metal.

Then, as suddenly as it had begun, it ended.

Frank wondered, once again, if this was normal for earthquakes. He sure hoped so. If it wasn't, some evil force was at work here.

He preferred to deal with Mother Nature.

"Why'd you grab me like that, Tom?" he asked. "You scared me half to death."

"Sorry, Frank," Tom said, "I didn't want you to get stabbed by the gate."

"Thanks, I guess," Frank said. "Let's just get you those sneakers already."

Frank looked back through the gate. The sneakers had fallen off his foot within easy reach. He stuck his hand through the bars to grab them.

"Ouch!" he screamed.

Chapter Twenty-One

"What happened?" Tom asked, his voice sounding thin and scared. "What are you yelling about?"

"I don't know," Frank said. "It felt like something bit me."

Frank looked at his right hand. He saw tooth marks on his skin. The skin hadn't been broken, but he had clearly been bitten by something.

"What could have bitten you?" Tom asked. "I didn't see anything in there but shoes."

Frank rubbed his hand. Gradually, the teeth marks began to fade. Then he remembered the shoes he had been trying to get for Tom.

They lay right on the other side of the gate now. He peered into the shoe store. He saw no sign of anything alive. Nothing moved.

Even so, there was no way he was going to stick his bare hand through the gate again. Even if he couldn't see anything, he didn't want to take any chances.

He picked up his own shoe, stuck his hand inside it, and used it as a shield. He reached through the gate to get the new shoes.

Even inside the shoe, his hand trembled as he remembered the bite he had suffered a moment earlier.

Carefully, his eyes open wide, he reached for the shoes. Beads of sweat stood out on his forehead.

He hooked the shoe that covered his hand on the laces that bound the new shoes together, and gingerly dragged them back through the grate.

Then he breathed a sigh of relief.

"Got 'em," he said.

He put his shoe back on, and Tom put on the new shoes. They seemed to fit well.

They were just standing up when, suddenly, they heard it again.

Padded footsteps.

"Listen," Frank said. "Did you hear that?"

They paused for a moment, holding their breath and listening. They clearly heard the sounds of scurrying.

"Maybe whatever bit you is running away," Tom said.

"Sounds like more than one little animal," Frank said.

"Maybe it's one big animal," said Tom.

But Frank disagreed. The tooth marks on his hand had been small and close together. They couldn't have been made by a large animal.

Still, he felt threatened. He didn't like being bitten by something he could not see. He didn't care for the dark, he didn't care for being trapped — in fact, he didn't care for the whole situation.

He felt his heartbeat start to race.

Calm down, he told himself. You can't panic. You've got a little brother to take care of.

He took Tom's hand and led him away from the shoe store and towards the staircase.

As they walked, Frank racked his brain, trying to think of a logical explanation for the bite.

"I've got it!" he shouted. His voice echoed through the abandoned mall, bouncing off the walls and down the corridors.

"Got what?" Tom asked, startled.

"I know how I got bitten," Frank said.

"How?"

"This mall has a pet store, doesn't it?" Frank said.

"Yeah," said Tom, "Mom took me there once. They had great lizards and snakes and frogs. They had this one really cool . . . "

"Some other time, Tom," Frank interrupted.

"Which way is the pet store? Do you remember?"

"I think it's by the stairs on the first level. But why?"

"I think maybe some pets have escaped," Frank said. "If what I'm thinking is right, there may be animals running loose all over this mall."

"How could that be?" asked Tom.

"Well, what if the earthquakes also messed with the electrical system in the pet store?" Frank asked. "What if the cages and gates at the pet store have been opening and closing just like all the other ones?"

"That could mean animals everywhere!" said Tom. "It would be like a great big petting zoo!"

"Not really that great, actually," said Frank.

"Why not?" Tom asked. "You like animals, too."

It was true. Frank was a real animal lover.

Back in Massachusetts when they were much younger, their family had lived on a farm. They had kept all kinds of animals — a pig, a donkey, some sheep, and a few chickens.

Of course they had dogs and a cat, too.

Farm animals and pets were one thing. But Frank thought that mysterious animals that you couldn't see, animals that bit your hand when you were trapped in a mall — well, that was a horse of a different color.

"Come on, Tom," he said. "Let's go see if the animals are on the loose."

"Even if there are animals roaming around, why would one bite you?" Tom asked. "That store only has harmless pets."

"Even harmless pets could get spooked by the earthquakes," Frank said. "If you were frightened and suddenly let loose in the mall, you might bite me too."

"Don't give me any ideas," said Tom.

Chapter Twenty-Two

Frank and Tom made their way to the staircase that would lead them back down to the first level of the mall.

For some reason, the mall seemed darker than it had been. Maybe the last shake of the earth had turned off some of the emergency lights.

Frank was really worried.

They'd had some pretty close calls. Neither of them had been really hurt, so far, but the night wasn't over, and they were no closer to getting out of the mall.

He thought about Deanna. He hoped she had made it home OK. He wondered if she was mad at him for not following after her.

Why hadn't he followed her, he asked himself angrily.

If only he had grabbed Tom and followed Deanna into the crowd of people pushing out the theater doors! They would probably be safe at home by now. Why hadn't he?

He knew exactly why, but the reasons seemed absurd now.

He hadn't charged into the crowd because he had wanted to seem brave and sensible. He had wanted to impress Deanna with his courage and his calm reaction to a crisis.

He had always been told never to panic in an emergency. He had thought he was doing the sensible thing by finding an alternate way out of the theater. He had thought he was saving his little brother from getting crushed by the crowds.

Now, instead of calm and brave, he felt scared and foolish.

Instead of impressing Deanna, he had gotten himself and Tom into the biggest mess of their lives.

He thought about his parents. He couldn't even *imagine* how mad they were going to be when they found out about this.

Frank was pretty sure at this point that they would find out. It was almost eleven o'clock.

His parents had said they'd be home early. He hoped they were having a really great time. Maybe they would even stay out all night!

No way. No matter how good a time they were

having, he knew his parents were far too responsible to stay out all night. Darn it.

Frank forced all thoughts of Deanna and his parents from his mind. He had to focus on getting out of this mall.

By the time the boys reached the staircase, the mall was even darker. All the lights had cut off. All they had to guide them was moonlight filtering through some skylights in the ceiling.

Slowly, carefully, Frank and Tom inched their way down the staircase. Frank grasped the handrail tightly. Tom grasped Frank even tighter than that.

"Tom," said Frank, "you're cutting off my circulation."

"Sorry, I'm just a little nervous." Tom let go of Frank's arm and continued to feel his way down the steps.

"Which way is the pet shop?" Frank asked.

"I'm not sure," Tom said. "It all looks different in the daytime and I've only been here a couple of times."

"Try to remember, would you?"

"I know!" Tom said. "Mom and I were coming down the escalator when I saw a puppy in the window. It must be down the corridor back over by the escalators!"

"Let's go," said Frank. "But don't even think about going near those escalators again. OK?"

"Don't worry about me," Tom replied firmly. "I may never take an escalator again for the rest of my life."

Chapter Twenty-Three

As Frank and Tom got closer to the escalators, they heard the footsteps again, muffled, padded, scurrying.

Except they sounded louder now. And there were more of them.

"Quit grabbing me so tightly, Tom," Frank said. "You're squeezing my arm too tight."

"I'm not even touching you!" Tom exclaimed, sounding hurt at being falsely accused.

Frank glanced down at his arm. It felt like Tom was giving him one of those twisting do-it-yourself sunburns.

What he saw stopped him in his tracks and sent shivers up his spine.

Coiled tightly around his forearm was a snake!

It looked like a boa constrictor. His friend Matt, back in Massachusetts, used to have one. He knew they weren't poisonous.

But he also knew they killed their prey by squeezing it to death.

Matt's snake had been a harmless family pet. This snake had an evil look. It stared right into Frank's eyes. It looked as if it was ready to sink its teeth into Frank's face.

In a flash, Frank slammed his arm into a storefront gate.

"Ow-w-w!" Frank screamed out in pain. He slammed his arm into the gate, again and again and again, trying to smash the snake off his arm.

"Are you nuts, Frank? Why'd you do that?" Tom yelled.

Finally, the snake loosed its grip, fell to the floor, and slithered away in the dim light of the moon.

Frank watched, his chest heaving, as the snake slid into the store beyond the gate. Its eyes gleamed in the darkness.

Clutching his arm, Frank limped away from the storefront towards Tom, who had stood frozen with fear during the entire episode.

"You OK?" Frank asked huskily.

"I'm OK," Tom squeaked. "How's your arm?"

"Sore," said Frank.

"It looked like the snake Matt used to have," Tom

said. "Except this one looked mean."

"It did look like Matt's snake," said Frank. "The only difference is, Matt's snake wouldn't hurt a fly. This one was out to kill."

"I guess you were right," said Tom. "The pet shop animals must have gotten loose."

"I guess so," said Frank, "but why are they acting so vicious?"

"Maybe the kids at school were right," said Tom.

"Right about what?" asked Frank.

"Maybe this mall *is* haunted."

Chapter Twenty-Four

Frank wasn't so sure he wanted to go anywhere near the pet shop anymore. In fact, he thought he'd rather not.

Clearly, pets were on the loose. *Mean* pets. That was all he needed to know, thank you very much.

He took Tom's hand, figured out in which direction the pet shop lay — and headed the other way.

Darkness shrouded them. They could barely see where they were going.

They heard no other footsteps now, only their own echoing hollowly through the eerie, empty mall.

They crossed under the escalators. Frank walked smack into a portable sign he hadn't seen, and knocked it over with a clatter that made them both jump.

They looked up and found themselves in front of a computer and electronics store.

Oddly enough, the gate was open.

"Should we go in?" Tom asked.

Frank peered into the store. He couldn't believe his eyes. This store looked just like the video arcade. All the computers were running.

"I think we should go in and find a phone," he said. "We need help. Big time. We'll never get out of here on our own."

He looked at his torn clothes and bruised arm. He thought of the melted pennies, the vicious animals and the bizarre escalator ride. He felt defeated.

And very, very scared. Absolutely *anything*, he felt, could happen next. And what happened next could be even worse — perhaps fatal. Without help, they might never get out at all.

"Let's go in," he said. "But don't touch anything, OK?"

Tom nodded.

Beeps and blips sounded from various computers. The two boys threaded their way between the noisy machines as they made their way to the back of the store.

There's always a phone at the cashier's desk, Frank thought. We'll just dial 9-1-1 and get help.

Calling 9-1-1 seemed justified. They had no other options. And Frank couldn't imagine being in any more trouble than they were in already.

But that was trouble enough. He had broken his

parents' cardinal rule — never leave the house when you are home alone at night.

Unless, of course, the house was on fire.

Maybe the house burned down while they were gone, Frank thought. That would save him from punishment.

Yeah, right.

Frank knew he had to clear his mind. All these thoughts were not helping him at all. He would have time enough to worry later.

They got to the back of the store and found the cashier's desk. It was very dark in the rear of the store, inky black. The boys couldn't even see each other.

Frank patted a desk, ran his hand over some papers, and felt a computer terminal that winked eerily at him with a pulsing green cursor.

Then, on a shelf under the computer, he felt the phone.

He lifted the receiver. There was no dial tone.

Could the phones be dead?

He remembered using the telephone at his dad's office. You had to dial "9" to get an outside line.

He felt the numbers on the phone, counting his way over and down. He pressed the button he thought was the "9."

The number "9" appeared on the computer screen.

Frank listened at the receiver. Still no dial tone.

He tried pressing "0" for the operator.

A zero appeared on the screen.

This was weird. Could the computer, Frank wondered, be dialing the phone for him? He still heard no dial tone.

"Hey, Frank," Tom whispered. "Check this out."

"What?"

"Every computer in the place," said Tom, "has the numbers nine and zero repeating all over the screens."

"I just dialed those two numbers," Frank said.

"Well, I think maybe you are calling the other computers."

"Let me try one more thing," said Frank.

He felt around the computer by the telephone, trying to find the power switch.

He found it, pressed it, and turned off the power. The screen went dark.

He picked up the receiver and heard a dial tone.

Success!

Quickly, he pressed 9-1-1.

Chapter Twenty-Five

Frank waited for the phone to ring and the police dispatcher to answer. He heard nothing but silence.

Then he heard Tom scream.

Frank jumped from behind the cashier's desk and ran to Tom, who stood staring at a computer screen.

He wasn't screaming anymore. He was frozen with fear.

Frank grabbed Tom gently by the shoulders.

"What's wrong?" he asked.

Tom didn't answer. His eyes were fixed on the screen.

"Tom, talk to me."

Still, Tom made no reply. Frank looked at the screen and his mouth fell open. What he saw sent chills up and down his spine.

The top of the screen had a message running across it.

It read "*9-1-1 can't help you now. 9-1-1 can't help you now.*" The message repeated over and over again.

At the bottom of the screen, a game of Animal Pursuit was being played. Frank recognized it because it was Tom's favorite computer game.

But this version looked different. Instead of animals going through mazes, trying to escape their predators, two boys ran through the mazes, pursued by animals.

All of the animals were after the boys!

Even the lowest animals on the food chain participated in the chase.

Something else looked different about this game of Animal Pursuit, too, but Frank couldn't put his finger one it.

"L-l-look," Tom stuttered, finally able to speak. "The maze — i-it's the m-m-mall."

Frank stared at the computer screen. How could it be?

The two figures moving through the maze wore the same color shirts that he and Tom had on.

On a hunch, Frank reached down to the keyboard and pressed the left arrow key. The screen changed to show where the boys had just been.

Sure enough, the image on the screen showed the staircase down from level two. It also showed a snake slithering in the store by the stairs.

"There's the snake that attacked your arm!" Tom shouted.

Frank hit the left arrow again.

The image switched to the upper level of the mall. Just inside the gate of the athletic shoe store he saw the image of a guinea pig.

So *that* was what had bitten him!

But why, he wondered, would a normally harmless creature bite?

Frank felt sure that the computer held the answers. He also felt sure that it held their only hope of escaping this madness.

"Tom, you know this game better than I do," he said. "Does it ever give you clues? I mean, if you're stuck in a maze, can you click on something that will show you the way out?"

"It doesn't work that way," Tom said. "First of all, *I'm* not usually in the maze. Animals are chasing other animals, instead of chasing me. Second of all, you can see where the predators are hiding before you get there, so you try to choose a path that leads away from them."

Frank reached down to the keyboard. This time he

planned to press the right arrow key. He hoped this would show him what lay in store for them.

He hesitated with his finger poised above the key.

He felt afraid of what he was about to see. This would be like looking into a crystal ball. Yesterday, if someone had offered him a look into the future, he would have jumped at the chance.

Now he was terrified.

He took a deep breath and pressed the key. It took a moment for the image on the screen to change.

When it did, Frank and Tom stopped, stared, and let out a gasp.

Chapter Twenty-Six

Frank looked at the image on the screen and felt his heart sink.

Around every corner, in almost every store, animals lurked.

All of them seemed to be at the low end of the food chain. If this had been the regular version of Animal Pursuit, the one Tom played at home, this would have been good news. In the real Animal Pursuit, you only had to worry about animals that were higher on the food chain than you.

There were no people in the real game. But if there had been, they would have been safe, because man is at the very top of the food chain.

But in this mad mall version, even the lowly guinea pigs were to be feared.

And they were everywhere. Mice, too. And dogs, cats, lizards, turtles. Every seemingly harmless pet was on the loose and not to be trusted.

"There *must* be a way out," Frank said. "Think, Tom — what help does the game give you?"

"Well, let's say you choose to be a fox in one game," Tom said. "You click on this and it shows you which animals are your predators, and which ones you can kill as you go through the maze."

Tom took the mouse and clicked on the help bar. The screen changed.

Now they saw a chart showing the food chain in this game.

The two figures of the boys were listed as prey. Every animal in the game — *every single one* — showed up as a predator.

"I don't believe this!" Frank shouted. "We're not safe from anything! Every animal out there is after us!"

Tom looked terrified. Frank knew he had to do something fast.

"What if we just quit the game?" he asked.

"I'll try it," Tom said. He moved the mouse back to the help bar and clicked on "quit."

In a moment, a small box of type appeared on the screen.

It read, "*Request Denied.*"

"It won't let us quit!" Tom whined. "This is *crazy*!"

"Let's try to restart the game," said Frank, "Go back to the help bar and select a new game."

The same box of type appeared — *"Request Denied."*

Frank reached down and pressed the power button. Perhaps with no power, the game would have to end.

The computer screen went blank. Frank breathed a sigh of relief. Tom looked like he might cry, he was so relieved. The game was over. Their ordeal had ended.

Then the screen clicked back to life. Another box of type appeared.

"Revenge is ours," it read. *"You must play the game!"*

Frank sagged with despair. Nothing he tried worked.

"This is totally creepy," Tom squeaked, his voice trembling. "Why would anybody want revenge against *us*?"

"What if the kids at school were right?" Frank asked. "What if the mall really *is* haunted by the ghosts of the dead animals from the pet cemetery?"

"I thought you didn't believe in ghosts," said Tom, sounding quavery and unsteady. "There is no such thing, right?"

"Well, I didn't believe in possessed computers either," Frank said. "But there's one right in front of me."

"Even if there *are* ghosts," Tom said, "why would they want revenge against *us*? *We* didn't do anything to them."

"No we didn't," said Frank. "But Dad might have."

"Dad?" Tom echoed. "What did *he* do?"

"He was one of the chief engineers when this mall was built," Frank replied.

"So you think maybe the ghosts of the animals are mad at him?"

"Could be," Frank said. "Although, Dad said the animal graves were moved to another pet cemetery before he joined the project."

"That's what the other people *told* Dad," Tom said. "What if they lied?"

"If they lied, then they brought Dad out to California under false pretenses," Frank said. "If Dad had known the truth, he wouldn't have taken this job. Maybe we would never have moved."

Now, besides feeling scared, Frank felt really mad. Building a mall on top of dead animals was bad enough. Forcing a kid to move all the way across the country by lying to his dad was unforgivable.

They had messed up his life. And now look at the trouble he was in.

Chapter Twenty-Seven

Frank checked his watch. It was eleven-thirty.

If his parents were home — and they probably were — they'd be worried sick. Worrying his parents was as bad as breaking rules.

He simply *had* to get out of this mess. And fast.

If only he had left his parents a note explaining where he had gone.

A note!

Why hadn't he thought of that before? With all these computers running, he could try to send an e-mail to his computer at home.

When his parents got home, maybe they would see it! His dad usually played on the computer every night before he went to bed. It was worth a shot.

Frank went back to the computer by the cashier's desk. He knew this one was definitely hooked to the phone lines. Maybe he could get on-line and send his dad an e-mail.

He clicked the power button. The screen glimmered to life. At the bottom, he saw an Internet icon.

He double-clicked it and entered his own password. The computer began dialing.

Moments later, he was connected to the net! He typed in his dad's e-mail address and then a message:

"*Dad —*

"*We are in trouble – trapped in the mall. Animals have gone mad. Need help to get out. Please come – HURRY!*

"*F. & T.*"

Frank sent the message. Now all they could do was hunker down and wait.

At least they had some candy to munch on. Frank suddenly realized how hungry he was. All this adventure and excitement had given him quite an appetite.

"Hey, Tom, I got a message out," he said. "Hopefully, help will be here soon. Let's have some of that candy."

He walked back over to where Tom stood watching the game screen.

"Frank," Tom said. "I have some bad news."

"What now?"

"On the screen here, the animals have started to move around outside the store," Tom said. "I don't think we're safe in here anymore."

This was not good. With the animals on the move, sitting and waiting for help seemed like a bad idea. A really bad idea.

"Oh, no," Frank said. "What if Dad doesn't see my message in time? We'd better try to get to another phone and call for help. The computer can't control *all* the phones in the mall."

"You want us to go out *there*, into the mall, and face those crazy animals?" Tom asked.

"We'll look ahead on the computer screen to see where the animals are hiding," Frank said. "And we'll try to avoid them."

"But there are so many of them," said Tom. "How will we keep track? Especially now that they are moving around?"

Frank thought for a moment. Then he got a brilliant idea.

He ran back to the cashier's desk and grabbed a set of keys he had noticed earlier. There were glass display cases around the store. Frank was betting the keys would open them.

He found a case displaying cellular phones and intercoms. At the back he saw a set of walkie-talkies.

Fumbling in the darkness, he tried one key after

another. None seemed to work. Most did not even fit in the lock.

Then, when he had nearly worked his way around the entire key ring, he found one that slipped easily into the lock. Gently, holding his breath, he turned it.

He heard a click. The door to the display case slid open.

He reached in and took out the walkie-talkies. A small light on the side showed that the batteries were charged.

Frank carried the radios over to Tom.

"Here's my idea," he began. "Listen carefully."

Tom stopped watching the screen and looked at Frank.

"OK," he said.

"You're much better at playing this game than I am," Frank said. "You've had far more experience. I want you to stay in the store and keep track of the game. I'm going to go into the mall to try to get to a pay phone. We can communicate with each other using the walkie-talkies. You'll see me move around the mall on the computer screen. Your job is to watch me, and radio me to let me know where the animals are."

"I get it!" Tom said, excitement creeping into his voice for the first time in hours. "I'll tell you where to walk and what to keep away from!"

"Will you be all right alone in the store?" Frank asked.

"Sure," Tom answered. "The real question is, will *you* be all right out *there*?"

Chapter Twenty-Eight

Frank picked up one of the walkie-talkies, walked to the far end of the store, and pressed the button.

"Hello," he said into the radio. "Testing, one, two, three . . ."

At the opposite end of the store, Tom's walkie-talkie squawked loudly. These were no cheap toys. Frank figured they probably had a really wide range.

"This is going to be so cool!" Tom said. "I feel like a spy."

"I feel like someone's next meal," Frank replied. "You have to take this seriously, Tom. I'm counting on you. My life will be in your hands."

The thought made him shiver.

"Don't worry, Frank, you can count on me," Tom said. "I'll talk you through the whole thing. I am really good at this game, you know."

Frank looked around for a weapon he could use if he needed one. He grabbed a big pair of scissors from the desk, shrugged, set his shoulders, stuck out his jaw, and walked out of the store.

He headed towards the movie theaters. He remembered having seen a pay phone in that area.

If the mall had seemed dark and creepy before, it seemed doubly so now. The light seemed dimmer, and the shadows seemed deeper.

He felt more nervous, being out in the mall all alone. Not that Tom had offered much protection. But at least he had been company.

The walkie-talkie crackled at his side.

"Frank, this is Tom, do you read me?"

Tom's voice came through the walkie-talkie crystal clear — and loud as all get-out.

"I read you," Frank said. "But just talk normally, OK?"

"There's a lot of action just ahead, so stay alert," said Tom.

"Don't worry, I wasn't planning on taking a nap."

"Duck, Frank, *NOW*!"

Frank hit the floor and covered his head with his hands just as a group of yellow birds whizzed past his head. In another second they would have flown right into his face.

When they were gone, Frank gathered himself and

retrieved the walkie-talkie from where it had clattered to the floor.

"Nice call, Tom" he panted into the radio. "You just saved me from a serious pecking."

"Well, watch out, because a cat is approaching the gate of the next store."

"There's a large planter to my left. Is it OK to go around it and avoid the cat?" Frank asked.

"I think so, but the planter seems to be full of mice," Tom replied. "Keep clear of it."

Cautiously, Frank skirted the planter, leaving a couple of feet between it and himself. He heard squeaking coming from under the plants. It sounded like a few harmless mice, but Frank knew better. Nothing here was harmless.

"Move left, Frank!" Tom shouted, sounding panicky. "Move left! *Jump*!"

Frank leapt to his left just as the mice started spilling over the side of the planter. Dozens of them scurried towards him, their eyes glowing yellow in the dim light of the mall.

"Now what, Tom?" Frank shouted into his walkie-talkie. "Where should I go?"

He had never thought he'd see the day when he was afraid of a few mice.

"Cut back around the planter and stay close to the gates," Tom's voice crackled over the radio. "The next few stores seem clear."

Frank ran around the far side of the planter and darted toward the gates. His heart pounded. Sweat dripped down his forehead. He couldn't remember the last time he had been this scared.

Oh, yes, he could.

The Halloween after he had turned nine years old, his dad had taken him to a haunted house. Tom had been too little to go along. It was supposed to be a special outing for just him and his dad.

The only thing Frank could remember was staring at a mannequin dressed as a witch and thinking how creepy she was.

She held a cleaver in her hand. Fake blood dripped down the blade. He had been mesmerized by the look in her eyes, and he had stood there, frozen and scared — when suddenly she sprang to life, raised the cleaver and shrieked at him.

Frank had run out of the haunted house crying. That had been the worst scare of his life.

Until tonight.

Being in this mall with mad animals was scarier. This was real. It was bizarre and hard to believe, but it was real. Frank had the bruises to prove it.

"Tom, I'm over by the gates of the clothing store," he said. "Is it clear?"

"You don't need to tell me your position, Frank," Tom said, sounding a little testy and self-important. "I can see you move on the computer screen. It's really cool."

"I'm so glad you're having fun," Frank replied. "Is the coast clear or not?"

For a moment, all Frank heard was silence.

"Tom?" Frank said into the radio. "Tom? Tom? Come in! Do you read me?"

Finally, the radio buzzed and hissed back to life, and Tom spoke.

"You're in big trouble now, Frank," he said.

Chapter Twenty-Nine

"What is it?" Frank shouted into the walkie-talkie. "What's happening?"

"A pack of dogs is coming!" Tom yelled. "Try climbing up the gate!"

Frank stuffed the walkie-talkie inside his shirt, stuck the scissors in his back pocket to free up his other hand, faced the gate of the clothing store, and started to pull himself up.

He was a good climber. He had strong arms. At school he was able to swing across the monkey bars, turn and swing back again.

The gates of this store had a crossbar four or five feet off the ground. He pulled himself up and used the crossbar as a foothold.

He clung to the bars of the gate and stood still on the crossbar. He saw another crossbar above his head, but he hoped he wouldn't have to go that high.

The silence was deadly. Frank heard nothing but

the sound of his own breathing.

Then he heard the dogs approaching.

It was so dark that they seemed to be one large object moving towards him. If Tom hadn't told him they were dogs, he never would have known.

He couldn't make out individual animals. He could see only a seething mass dotted with the flash of many yellow eyes, and studded with the glitter of a hundred sharp, white teeth.

The radio crackled.

"Can you see them yet Frank?" Tom asked.

Frank could hear Tom's voice coming from the walkie-talkie he had stuffed inside his shirt. But he couldn't let go of the gate to answer.

The dogs stopped and snarled below his feet. He made out about a dozen of them. Fortunately, the mall pet shop only sold puppies; these dogs seemed vicious but small. Even when they jumped, they could barely reach his feet.

A shaggy black and white one jumped, grabbed his left shoe, and refused to let go. The dog hung by its teeth, growling, trying to pull Frank off the gate.

This puppy was strong! He snarled and shook his head back and forth, trying to pry Frank from the gate.

Frank felt his grip loosening. He stuck his arms

100

through the gate, clasped his hands together and held on as tightly as he could.

The puppy held on tightly, too. Frank felt the dog's teeth tear through the side of his sneaker.

Bracing himself, Frank raised his leg. The dog dangled in mid-air. Frank swung his leg with all his might and smashed the dog into the gate.

The dog dropped to the ground with a whimper and scampered off into the darkness. Moments later, all the dogs retreated.

Frank stayed on the gate. He tried to catch his breath and calm himself down.

Suddenly, he became aware of Tom's voice.

"Come on, Frank, answer me," Tom asked frantically. "Are you OK? Frank? Frank?"

Frank let go of the gate with one hand and took the walkie-talkie out of his shirt.

"I'm OK, little brother," he said. "I'm OK."

"Why didn't you answer me?" Tom said, sounding near tears. "When I saw the dogs run away on the screen, and you didn't answer me, I thought you were dead!"

"I'm fine, Tom," Frank said. "I just couldn't get to my walkie-talkie. It's kind of hard to hold on to the gate and press the button to speak all at the same time."

"I guess it would be," Tom said. "So, were the dogs vicious?"

"Let's just say you wouldn't want to find one of them under your tree this Christmas," Frank replied.

Chapter Thirty

Tom assured Frank that it was safe to climb down off the gate — for the moment.

Frank could hardly catch his breath. His heart still pounded at twice its normal speed.

What a night this had turned out to be!

He knew he was getting closer to the pay phone. But he wondered whether he would make it all the way and call the police without first getting mauled by an insane pet? Would the phones even work?

Suddenly, he   felt very tired. He'd had quite a workout. And the mental stress — the worry, the fear, the horror of trying to survive — had exhausted him.

All he wanted to do was crawl into his nice warm bed and sleep for two days. Wouldn't it be great if this were nothing but a bad dream?

When scary books or movies turned out to be only a bad dream, Frank was always a little disappointed. But he wouldn't be disappointed now. Not in the least.

Tom's voice hissed through the walkie-talkie and brought him back to reality. Unfortunately, this was no dream.

"Frank, it's really weird," Tom said. "But the screen seems clear of any predators now."

"Does that ever happen in your game at home?" Frank asked.

"It happens either when you've gotten past all of the predators and you move on to the next level, or when you win the game," Tom said. "Maybe it's all over. Maybe we've won!"

"It doesn't seem possible," Frank said. "Why would they stop playing all of a sudden and let us win? I hate to say it but it seems more likely that we're moving onto a new level. And a new level is just what I don't need."

"I think you're right," Tom said.

"Why?" Frank asked. "What do you see now? What's happening?"

Frank waited for Tom to answer but he heard nothing.

"Tom? Tom?" he yelled into the radio. "Hey! What's up? Talk to me, Tom!"

"I . . . I . . . can't believe what I'm seeing," Tom stammered.

"Don't keep me in suspense!" Frank shouted. "Am I about to die or something?"

"The screen went blank for a moment and now it's like a whole new game is playing. There are even *more* animals then before. We must have moved onto the next level. A more difficult level."

"Do you think I can make it to the phone?" Frank asked.

"The phone isn't showing up on the computer so I can't be sure. Where is it exactly?"

Frank stuck his head out around the wall. He could just see the turn-off into the corridor where he thought the phone was.

He remembered having seen it just outside of the candy store. Why hadn't they used it then?

Frank knew the answer. That had been when he still thought they had a chance of escaping this whole mess and getting home before his parents did. If he had only known then what he knew now.

No time for regrets, he told himself. He needed to act. He pressed the button on his walkie-talkie.

"Tom, the phone is just around the next corner by the candy store," he said. "Does it look like I can make it?"

"It's going to be tough," replied Tom, "but I've

got an idea."

"What is it?"

"I'm going to try to move you with the computer," said Tom.

"*What*?" Frank screamed into the radio. "Are you *crazy*?"

"Listen to me for a minute, Frank," Tom said. "In my Animal Pursuit game at home I move the main character by clicking on the space ahead of it. If I am the fox, I click on the box ahead of the fox to move it forward or up or down. If I do the same for you, maybe you'll move faster and I'll be able to help you avoid the predators."

Frank didn't say a word. He was thinking about the wisdom of putting his fate, body and soul, into the hands of his eight-year-old brother. He was thinking about whether he would like being moved about without willing it, whether he would willingly relinquish control over his own movements to a kid with a cursor.

"Frank, are you there?" Tom asked. "Did you hear what I said?"

"I heard you," Frank said. "I'm thinking."

"Well, think fast" Tom said. "The animals are on the move."

"Do you really think it will work?" Frank asked. He tried to imagine himself moving without so much as twitching a muscle. It would be very weird.

Maybe *too* weird.

"I think it's worth a try," Tom said. "Remember, I'm really good at this game at home."

"I know you are," Frank said. "But this is my *life* we're talking about."

"I'll just play like I'm going for an all-time high score," Tom said.

"No, thanks," Frank radioed back. "Just play like my life depends on it."

<u>Chapter Thirty-One</u>

Frank had never felt so strange in all his life.

His feet barely touched the ground. He felt an invisible force jerk his body from left to right and then back again.

Each time he moved, a different animal whizzed by. He narrowly avoided a pack of snapping turtles with the largest jaws he had ever seen.

Next he felt himself jerked sharply upward as, beneath his feet, clattered hamsters with claws as sharp as knives.

Frank flew around the perimeter of the fountain. The beautiful lights still blazed red and blue. From up here, Frank could see down into the water.

What he saw filled him with horror.

Hundreds of fish filled the fountain. Fish of all colors swam and flipped and jumped. He couldn't tell if the lights made the water colorful, or the fish did. Or perhaps the lights made the fish *appear* colorful.

Whichever it was, the beauty was deceptive. The fish were in a feeding frenzy. Frank looked down, and his blood ran cold.

The fish were eating each other alive!

Every second or two, another fish would jump out of the water and snap at the air. Frank's feet dangled perilously close to the water. He bent his knees to raise his legs higher, and prayed that Tom would whisk him away safely.

The fish leapt and snapped and splashed. The radio crackled.

"How are you doing, Frank?" Tom asked.

"I feel like I'm on an amusement park ride that's broken," replied Frank. "I'm getting sick to my stomach."

"Well, I can't stop moving you around now," Tom said. "Snakes and lizards are waiting for you down this last corridor."

With that, Frank's body jolted around the corner into the final hallway. The ground below him seemed to move and twist and seethe.

The floor of the corridor was completely covered in snakes.

"There's not a clear place in sight!" Frank screamed into the walkie-talkie. "How will I get to the phone?"

"Don't worry, Frank," Tom replied. "I've got it under control."

What happened next was a blur to Frank. He moved so quickly he could not see where he was going or where he had been.

The next thing he knew he was perched on top of the pay phone booth.

"I'm here!" he shouted. "You did it, little brother!" He felt enormously relieved to be resting on something solid, rather than suspended in mid-air.

He was so relieved he wanted to throw up or pee or sleep or something.

"I just had to get you all the way past the snakes, then I was able to send you back to the phone," Tom said. "On this level, once you get past a predator, it disappears."

Frank looked down. Every single snake was gone!

He jumped down from his perch and grabbed the phone.

Yes! There was a dial tone.

Quickly, he pressed 9-1-1.

After only one ring, he heard a voice on the other end.

"This is 9-1-1. Is this an emergency?"

Frank hadn't even thought of what he would say.

If he told the dispatcher that mad animals were after him, she would probably think he was a prankster and hang up. He figured it was better to leave that part out and stick to the basics.

"Yes," he said. "It sure is. My brother and I are locked in the mall. We were at the movies during the earthquake and we went out the emergency exit and got locked in. Please . . . "

Suddenly, Frank felt the phone get ripped from his hand. His body jerked backwards, away from the phone.

"Tom!" he shouted into the walkie-talkie. "What the heck's going on?"

"Sorry, Frank," Tom's voice replied. "I had to move you. Those lizards were closing in."

Frank looked back at the dangling receiver. The phone was crawling with lizards.

"Hopefully, the operator got enough information to send help," Frank said. "Where are you taking me?"

"I think you should come back here," Tom said matter-of-factly as Frank continued whizzing down the corridor. "It seems to be the safest place right now."

Frank flew through the mall, zigging this way and zagging that, until he landed back at the computer store.

"What a way to travel!" he exclaimed as his feet touched the ground. "Nobody is going to believe this."

"If we live to tell about it," said Tom. He looked scared and his voice trembled.

"Don't lose hope on me now, little brother," Frank said. "You saved my skin out there, you know. I'll never tease you about playing computer games again."

Just then, the boys heard a strange noise. It sounded like a motor running. Actually, it sounded like many motors running.

The boys ran to the front of the store just as the gate came down. Before they could think, instinct told them to run out.

The gate crashed shut behind them.

Chapter Thirty-Two

"Oh, *no!*" Frank wailed. "*Now* what do we do?"

Without the computer screen, he and Tom had no way of knowing what lay in store for them. They couldn't see where the animals were hiding, they wouldn't know what lurked around the next corner, and they had no idea what would strike next.

Then, softy at first, they began hearing strange noises. They sounded faint and far-away, but with each passing minute they grew louder and louder.

Frank and Tom couldn't see any creatures, but they could feel their presence. They *had* to get out of the mall.

But how?

"I've got it!" Frank yelled. "What if we go back into hallways behind the movie theater? We didn't see any animals in there."

"It's worth a try, I guess," Tom said.

"It's better than standing around here waiting to

get mauled to death," said Frank. "Let's go!"

They moved through the mall carefully, peering around corners, then darting to a new place of safety. They tried to stay away from the gates, planters, fountains and other structures. They assumed animals could be concealed everywhere.

The noises grew louder. It sounded as if the animals were furious. Tom stopped in his tracks and started to shiver.

Frank put his arm around Tom and practically shoved him along.

With each step they took, a small animal scurried toward them. Frank was no longer walking but stomping and kicking and jumping.

Out of nowhere, a cat sprang at them.

Tom screamed and buried his face in Frank's chest. The cat clung to the leg of Frank's jeans. He felt its claws tear through the denim to his skin.

The cat bared its teeth and hissed. It looked ready to scratch out Frank's eyes.

Suddenly, Frank remembered the scissors. They were still tucked into the back pocket of his jeans.

In a split second, before he even had time to think, Frank reached for the scissors and jabbed them down hard into the cat's back.

The screech that followed was unbelievable. Frank had never heard such a sound in his life.

He pulled the scissors back. The cat fell to the ground. Frank was sure it was dead.

But it was not. Frank watched as the cat cowered away into the darkness.

Frank looked at the weapon he held in his trembling hand. It was perfectly clean and shiny.

How could that be?

He had just stabbed the scissors deep into a cat. He had felt them plunge into the cat's body. He had heard the cat screech in pain.

How could it be that the scissors were not covered with blood?

"Is it over?" asked Tom. His voice was so tiny, Frank barely heard him.

"It's over," Frank said. "The cat is gone."

"That was so scary," Tom squeaked. He was shaking all over. "When I was in the computer store and you were out here alone, it didn't even seem real. I practically convinced myself that I was just playing a game."

"Well, it may be a game," Frank said. "But it's a deadly one."

"I can't take much more of this," Tom whined.

"We've got to keep going," Frank said. "A moving target is harder to hit."

That was all Tom needed to hear. He started walking again at once.

Frank kept his arm around his little brother as they moved toward the exit.

It was in sight! Just a few more yards and they would escape into the safety of the back hallways on the other side of the emergency doors.

But would they really be safe?

There was only one way to know for sure.

Chapter Thirty-Three

Frank and Tom continued walking towards the door that led to the interior hallways. A few more steps and they would be there.

They didn't make it.

Just outside of the door, a circle of moonlight shone on the floor. Frank was drawn into it. He didn't even remember stepping that way. His movements felt completely out of his control.

"W-what's happening?" Tom asked. He was walking towards the pool of moonlight, too.

Clutching one another, the brothers stepped into the center of the circle, fell silent and took in their surroundings.

On the edge of the ring of light stood the animals. Hundreds of them.

There were puppies, cats, guinea pigs, snakes, lizards, turtles, mice and birds. Every creature had wicked yellow eyes that gleamed in the darkness. Thousands of pointy white teeth shone in the eerie moonlit glow.

The boys were surrounded.

The animals were all screeching and growling and hissing at them. The sounds alone terrified Frank. He felt his knees start to buckle.

Slowly, almost imperceptibly, the animals began to creep forward.

"We're going to die!" Tom wailed.

Frank could feel his brother's body shaking madly. A pair of scissors wasn't going to help them now.

Frank stamped his feet at the approaching horde.

Still they advanced.

He shouted and waved his arms and kicked at the animals.

Still they advanced.

Tom started crying. Frank felt despair overwhelm him. He had no more ideas.

He imagined the headline in the newspaper: *"Two brothers found mutilated in the mall — story on page two."*

He braced himself for the attack.

Suddenly, lights blazed on all over the mall. Bright lights! Hundreds of them. The boys blinked and shut their eyes in the sudden glare.

Then they heard the sweetest sound they'd ever

heard in their lives.

"Frank! Tom! Where are you?"

It was their dad!

The boys were stunned. Neither one could speak. They stood clutching one another, frozen where they stood just outside the emergency exit.

Suddenly, the door burst open and their father charged into the room!

Tom broke away from Frank and ran into his father's arms.

That's when Frank noticed it. The animals were gone. Vanished. All of them.

There wasn't a trace of an animal anywhere.

Chapter Thirty-Four

"Are you boys OK?" Mr. Chase asked. "You gave your mother and me quite a scare!"

Two police officers stood next to their dad, looking bored.

"We're OK," Frank said.

Tom still had his face buried in his dad's chest. It looked as if he might never let go.

"You don't look so good, Frank," said his dad. "You look like you've just seen a ghost."

Frank didn't know what to say. Would anybody believe him if he told them what had happened to them in the mall tonight? Then he remembered — he had the torn clothes and bruises to prove it.

He looked down at his clothes. The holes in his jeans were gone! His sneakers were no longer full of teeth marks. He had no bruises on his arms.

Frank looked at Tom. He was wearing his old

sneakers! Both of them! Even the one that had been crushed by the escalator.

This was unbelievable. It was like it never happened. But Frank *knew* that it had. This was too weird.

Mr. Chase tried to pry his younger son off him.

"Let me have a look at you, Tom," he said. "Are you OK?"

"No I'm not OK," Tom shouted. "We almost got killed here tonight. We were attacked by wild animals and there were earthquakes and the fountain is filled with acid or man-eating fish or something! The whole mall is *haunted*!"

"Slow down there, son" said one of the police officers. "You aren't making any sense."

"What's he talking about, Frank?" asked Mr. Chase. "What have you two been up to?"

Frank had to think fast. Should he tell the truth and risk having everyone think he was a lunatic?

Clearly, they all thought Tom was out of his mind. Would it change anything to speak up about all the strange things that happened here tonight?

Probably not.

One thing was sure — he was going to be in big trouble no matter what. Why have his parents think he was lying, on top of everything else?

"You have a lot of explaining to do, young man," said Mr. Chase.

It was never a good sign when his dad called him young man. Whatever the punishment was going to be, after a night like tonight, he could take anything his parents could dish out.

"I'll explain it all to you on the way home, Dad. Can we just go? I think Tom will calm down as soon as we get out of here."

Frank and Tom followed their dad through the door into the interior hallways. Bright lights blazed up and down the hall. Everything looked so much safer in the light.

It felt so much safer to have Dad there.

Frank began thinking that maybe his imagination *had* run away with him. Maybe none of it really did happen. Maybe the movie they had seen had played games with his mind.

That had to be it. None of this could happen in real life. It was crazy.

They walked out into the cool night air. Frank took a deep breath and savored the sweetness of the night.

It must have all been my imagination, he thought. After all, there can be no logical, scientific explanation for all that has happened.

But as Frank went to sit in the front seat of his dad's car, he felt a stab in the back of his leg. He reached around to his back pocket and pulled out the scissors he had taken from the computer store.

The scissors were covered with blood.